Put Beginning Readers on the Right Track with
ALL ABOARD READING™

The All Aboard Reading series is especially designed for beginning readers. Written by noted authors and illustrated in full color, these are books that children really want to read—books to excite their imagination, expand their interests, make them laugh, and support their feelings. With fiction and nonfiction stories that are high interest and curriculum-related, All Aboard Reading books offer something for every young reader. And with four different reading levels, the All Aboard Reading series lets you choose which books are most appropriate for your children and their growing abilities.

Picture Readers

Picture Readers have super-simple texts, with many nouns appearing as rebus pictures. At the end of each book are 24 flash cards—on one side is a rebus picture; on the other side is the written-out word.

Station Stop 1

Station Stop 1 books are best for children who have just begun to read. Simple words and big type make these early reading experiences more comfortable. Picture clues help children to figure out the words on the page. Lots of repetition throughout the text helps children to predict the next word or phrase—an essential step in developing word recognition.

Station Stop 2

Station Stop 2 books are written specifically for children who are reading with help. Short sentences make it easier for early readers to understand what they are reading. Simple plots and simple dialogue help children with reading comprehension.

Station Stop 3

Station Stop 3 books are perfect for children who are reading alone. With longer text and harder words, these books appeal to children who have mastered basic reading skills. More complex stories captivate children who are ready for more challenging books.

In addition to All Aboard Reading books, look for All Aboard Math Readers™ (fiction stories that teach math concepts children are learning in school) and All Aboard Science Readers™ (nonfiction books that explore the most fascinating science topics in age-appropriate language).

All Aboard for happy reading!

To Lyndsey—J.D.

To my husband, Dorrance—L.H.

Library of Congress Cataloging-in-Publication Data

Dussling, Jennifer.
    Anne of Green Gables / adapted from L.M.Montgomery's Anne of Green Gables by
Jennifer Dussling ; illustrated by Lydia Halverson.
        p. cm.—(All aboard reading. Level 3)
    Summary: Anne, an eleven-year-old orphan, is sent by mistake to live with a lonely,
middle-aged brother and sister on a Prince Edward Island farm and proceeds to make an
indelible impression on everyone around her.
    [1. Orphans—Fiction. 2. Friendship—Fiction. 3. Country life—Prince Edward Island—
Fiction. 4. Prince Edward Island—Fiction.] I. Halverson, Lydia, ill. II. Montgomery, L.M.
(Lucy Maud), 1874-1942. Anne of Green Gables. III. Title. IV. Series.
PZ7.D943 An 2000
[E]—dc21

00-049591

ISBN   0-448-42459-2   D E F G H I J

No! It wasn't. It was only two o'clock. Anne flew off to the picnic. She and Diana won a three-legged race—against the boys. She rowed on the lake. And she ate a big scoop of ice cream. Meanwhile, Marilla admitted to Matthew what had happened. "I've learned a lesson," she said. "Anne is hard to understand. But she'll turn out all right. And no home will be dull with her in it."

After that, Anne and Marilla got along better. Life at Green Gables was almost perfect, except for Anne's red hair.

"I can imagine away my freckles and green eyes and skinniness," Anne moaned to Matthew. "But I cannot imagine that red hair away." It was Anne's sore spot.

But the new boy at school, Gilbert Blythe, did not know that. Anne did not think much of Gilbert. The first time she saw him, he winked at her. He was used to all the girls liking him. He was very handsome.

One day, Anne was sitting at her desk looking out the window, dreaming as usual. Gilbert was trying to make Anne look at him. He made faces at her. But no luck.

Finally Gilbert picked up the end of Anne's long red braid and said, "Carrots! Carrots!"

Then Anne looked at him! She sprang to her feet. "You mean, hateful boy!" she cried.

And—thwack! Anne brought her slate down on Gilbert's head! The slate broke in two.

The teacher put a hand on Anne's shoulder. "What is going on?" he asked.

Anne said nothing. It was Gilbert who spoke. "It was my fault," he said. "I teased her."

The teacher did not care. He made Anne stand in front of the class for the rest of the day. He wrote, "Ann Shirley has a very bad temper" on the blackboard. He even spelled Anne's name wrong!

Anne did not cry. She was furious. This was Gilbert's fault. She would never, never forgive him!

And she didn't. Gilbert tried to say he was sorry. Anne walked right by. The next day, he gave her a candy heart. She ground it under her foot. "Iron has entered my soul," she told her friend Diana.

Anne's pride had a long memory. Sometimes Anne's pride led her into trouble. That was what happened the day of Diana's party.

The girls had tea. They played games. Soon they got bored. In the backyard, they started giving one another dares. First Carrie dared Ruby to climb a huge willow tree. Ruby was scared of the fat green caterpillars that lived there. She did it anyway.

Then Josie dared Jane to hop around
the garden on one leg. Jane tried. But
her leg gave out on the third corner.

Anne dared Josie to walk
along the top of the fence.
Josie walked it easily.
She gave Anne a
smug glance.

The look cut Anne through and through. She tossed her braids. "It's not so wonderful to walk a low fence," she sniffed. "I know a girl who walked the peak of a roof."

"I don't believe it," Josie said. "I dare you to try."

Anne turned pale. Walk the roof? She was scared. But her honor was at stake.

A ladder was leaning against Diana's house. In a minute, Anne scrambled up it.

Soon Anne was standing on top of the
roof. She started to walk along the peak.

After a few steps, disaster struck. Anne swayed. She lost her balance. She stumbled. She fell—sliding down the long roof and into the brush on the ground!

The girls rushed over. "Anne, are you killed?" Diana shrieked.

Anne sat up dizzily. "No, Diana, I am not killed," she said. "But my ankle!"

Diana's father was called for. He carried Anne back to Green Gables.

Anne's ankle was broken. It would take weeks for her ankle to heal. Anne would be stuck at home for seven long weeks.

"Isn't it lucky I have a good imagination?" Anne asked Marilla. "Some people have no imagination. What do they do when they break their bones?"

There were other times, however, when Anne's imagination was not a blessing.

The worst time was when Anne had the idea to act out a poem.

Anne, Diana, Jane, and Ruby loved to read poems. Their favorite poem was about a beautiful maiden named Elaine. Elaine died of love for Sir Lancelot. Then her body drifted in a boat to her lover's castle. All they needed to act out Elaine's death was the pond—and Diana's father's boat.

"Anne, you must be Elaine," Diana said.

"Elaine can't have red hair!" Anne cried. But no one else would do it. Diana and Ruby were too scared. Jane was too practical.

So Anne got into the boat. She lay back. She closed her eyes. Diana placed a blue flower in Anne's hands. The girls pushed the boat off. Anne drifted away.

For a few minutes, Anne enjoyed the scene. Then she felt a trickle of water. The boat was leaking!

Anne scrambled to her feet. The trickle became a river. The water in the boat covered her ankles. More and more water was leaking in. At this rate the boat would sink before Anne reached land!

The boat drifted toward a bridge.
Anne had only one chance. When it
passed a support, Anne grabbed it.
There was nowhere to go from there.
She was stuck. The boat drifted away
and promptly sank. Anne heard Jane,
Diana, and Ruby scream. She knew
help would come soon.

It was sooner than she imagined. Gilbert came rowing under the bridge!

He was shocked to see a familiar girl with red hair and big gray eyes looking down at him. "Anne Shirley! How did you get there?" he asked.

He pulled his boat close to Anne. He helped her in. Anne sat, furious and dripping. Of all people, why did Gilbert have to be the one to rescue her? Gilbert rowed to shore.

When they landed, Anne sprang out of the boat. Gilbert put a hand on her arm. "Anne," he said, "can't we be friends?"

Anne paused. The half-shy, half-eager look in Gilbert's eyes stopped her. Her heart gave a quick, queer little beat. Then the memory of the day in the school came rushing back to her.

"No," she said coldly.

"All right," Gilbert said, his face red. "I'll never ask you to be friends again."

She held her head high. Still, she almost wished she had given a different answer. Then she started on the path for home.

Home—that was truly what Green
Gables had become. It was Anne's home.
And almost before she knew it, two years
had gone by since the day Matthew
picked her up at the station.

One evening, Marilla put down her
knitting. She looked at Anne curled up on
the rug. Marilla had learned to love Anne
deeply. Now Marilla could not imagine
the place without her. And Matthew
adored Anne more than anyone.

"When we took you in," Marilla said,
"we promised to do our best for you."

Marilla and Matthew didn't have a lot of money. But still they wanted to pay for Anne to study to be a teacher.

It had been Anne's dream to become a teacher. "Oh, thank you." She flung her arms around Marilla. "I'm so grateful to you and Matthew."

Anne's heart was filled with joy. She had her family now. A family that included Marilla, Matthew, Diana, Jane, Ruby, all her friends, and all her neighbors.

Marilla hugged Anne back.
"Anne, you will always have a
home at Green Gables."

L.M. Montgomery's
Anne of Green Gables

Adapted by Jennifer Dussling
Illustrated by Lydia Halverson

Grosset & Dunlap • New York

Eleven-year-old Anne Shirley sat stiffly on top of some cartons at an empty train station. She clutched a shabby bag in her skinny hands. Two very thick, very red braids ran down her back. She had not moved for half an hour. Today was the most important day of her life.

Anne's big gray eyes watched as a man pulled up to the station in a buggy. Was this finally Matthew?

Anne was an orphan. Her parents had died when she was a baby. For years she had been passed from family to family. Finally she had ended up at a home for orphans. But today Anne was going to a real home, a house called Green Gables. Anne had been dreaming about this day for as long as she could remember. She was going to live there with Matthew Cuthbert and his sister Marilla. They had decided to take in an orphan child.

"Are you Mr. Matthew Cuthbert?"
Anne asked the man.

The man nodded. Then he said kindly,
"I'm sorry I was late. Come along."

Matthew was wearing a suit. But he
looked uncomfortable in it. He had gray
hair and a thick brown beard. Anne
thought he acted shy.

Anne chattered during the whole buggy ride. She was happy and excited. She couldn't help letting out those feelings in words. Matthew didn't say much, but Anne could tell he liked listening. Finally the buggy pulled up

to her new home, a perfect little place.
Green Gables was a snug wooden house
with white blooming cherry trees on
one side and a neat yard all around it.

"It seems like a dream," Anne said
joyfully. "But it _is_ real."

A tall, thin woman came to greet
them. She stopped in surprise. "Matthew,
where is the boy?" Marilla said sharply.
The words hit Anne hard.

In her mind Anne saw herself being
sent back to the orphanage. "You don't
want me?" Her voice trembled. Then she
threw herself into a chair and burst into
tears.

Marilla looked at Matthew helplessly.
She told Anne, "We need a boy to help
Matthew on the farm. But we won't turn
you out—not tonight anyway."

Anne was miserable. But she wiped away her tears. For the rest of the day, she worked hard and tried to do everything Marilla asked. She helped with dinner.

She washed the dishes—and dried them, too. Still, Marilla was firm. Anne would have to go back to the orphanage.

Matthew did not agree. He was quiet, but he liked Anne. "She's a real nice little thing, Marilla," he said. "It's a pity to send her back."

Anne could see that Marilla usually made most of the decisions. Yet by the end of the next day, Matthew convinced Marilla to let Anne stay at Green Gables for good. It was their duty to help this young girl. And although Marilla would not admit it, part of her admired Anne's spirit. Anne finally had a home.

Still, things were not easy. Marilla grew to like Anne more. But Anne wasn't like other girls her age. She talked all the time. She had such strange ideas.

"Wouldn't it be nice if roses could talk?" she asked Marilla on her second day there. "I'm sure they would tell us lovely things."

Marilla sniffed. "I don't believe in imagining things different from what they really are," she said. She was practical. Anne, on the other hand, was not.

She made friends and did well at her new school. But Anne was a dreamer. That often got her into trouble. Marilla didn't know what to make of her.

One Saturday morning, Marilla came down from her room. She looked upset.

Anne was shelling peas in the kitchen. But she was not thinking of peas. She was thinking of the church picnic. It was all she had talked about for a week. This would be her first picnic—ever! Her new friends Diana, Ruby, and Jane were going to be there. And there was going to be ice cream. Anne had never tasted ice cream before. Diana tried to explain it to her, but she still could not imagine it.

"Anne, did you see my purple pin?" Marilla asked.

"Yes, I saw it the other day," Anne said. Her mind was still on the picnic.

"Did you touch it?" Marilla didn't like anyone touching her things. But the pin was so lovely. The purple stone sparkled like a starry night.

"Y-e-s-s." Anne hurried to explain, "But I put it right back on the dresser where I found it."

"The pin is gone," Marilla said coldly.
"Tell me the truth. Did you lose it?"

Marilla hated lies. But Anne wasn't
lying. She met Marilla's look squarely.
"No, I didn't," she said.

Marilla did not believe her. "Go to
your room. Stay there until you are
ready to confess. I don't care how long
it takes."

"But I didn't do anything!" cried
Anne. "And the picnic—it's tomorrow!"

Marilla's face was as hard as stone.
"You won't go to the picnic until you
confess," she said sternly.

Anne stayed in her room. Matthew
tried to talk to Marilla. He knew that
Anne's heart was set on going to the
picnic. Marilla would not give in.

The next day dawned sunny and clear—perfect for a picnic. Anne couldn't miss the picnic. All her friends would be there. There was only one thing to do.

Marilla brought Anne's breakfast to her room. Anne was waiting for her. "Marilla, I'm ready to confess," she said. "I took the pin. I imagined I was a beautiful rich lady. I pinned it on my dress and went outside. On the bridge, I took it off to look at it. It slipped through my fingers. It sank for evermore in the lake."

Marilla was shocked. "Anne, you are a wicked girl!"

"Yes," Anne agreed. "Now can I go to the picnic?"

"Picnic! You're not going to any picnic!"

Anne sprang to her feet. "Marilla, you promised!" she said.

Marilla was firm. Now there was nothing Matthew could say. The morning passed in a dismal way. Marilla kept busy. She raked in the yard. Then she went up to fix a rip in her favorite black lace shawl.

Marilla picked up the shawl. The light struck something on the shawl, something purple and sparkly. Marilla gasped. It was the pin! All at once, Marilla remembered. She'd worn the shawl to church the other night and had laid it on the dresser when she had returned home.

Marilla went to Anne's room. "Anne! I just found my pin stuck on my black shawl. Why did you tell me that story?"

"You said I had to stay in my room until I confessed," Anne said wearily. "I confessed so I could go to the picnic."

Marilla sighed. Then all of a sudden she laughed. "Anne, I was wrong. If you forgive me, I'll forgive you for your lie. Now go get ready for the picnic."

Anne jumped up. "Isn't it too late?"